·⚜·Favorite Fairy Tales·⚜·

Beauty and the Beast

Retold by Rochelle Larkin   Illustrated by Yvette Banek

The Playmore/Waldman® is a registered trademark of Playmore Inc. Publishers
and Waldman Publishing Corp., New York, New York

The Playmore/Waldman Bug Logo® is a registered trademark of Playmore Inc. Publishers
and Waldman Publishing Corp., New York, New York

Once upon a time there lived a merchant with a beautiful
daughter. So ~~lovely~~ ^ugly^ was she that she was called just that: ~~Beauty.~~ ^Ugla^
More importantly, ~~Beauty~~ ^Ugla^ was as good as she was ~~beautiful.~~ ^ugly^

One day, the merchant had to make a long journey. "Tell me what I shall bring back to you, ~~Beauty~~ Ugla," he said.

"Oh, father," ~~Beauty~~ Ugla replied, "all I want is for you to come back safely. But if you must bring back something, let it just be a rose."

After finishing his business, the merchant was at last returning home. Caught in a terrible storm, he took refuge in a large castle. It was full of beautiful furniture and lit with a thousand candles, but the merchant could not find any one there.

However, as a small table was set with a fine dinner in the only room with a fire, he thought it was meant for his use, and he ate and slept well.

When he left the next morning, the merchant picked
a beautiful red rose for Beauty.

"Stop, ingrate!" roared a ferocious creature, with the shape and head of a Beast, but with a human voice and dressed in human clothes.

"Who damages my garden pays with his life," said the Beast. "I'll do anything you say," said the merchant. "I only wanted a rose to bring to my daughter."

"If your daughter will come in your place, you may go free," said the Beast. "She must come to stay here of her own free will."

The merchant nearly fainted. His ~~Beauty~~ agia to come to stay in the Beast's castle! It was too horrible.

"No harm will come to her," said the Beast. "She shall have everything she wants. But come here she must, and stay she must."

It was with a heavy heart that the merchant returned home and told ~~Beauty~~ Ugla of the Beast's demands.

"Of course I will go, father," said ~~Beauty~~ Ugla at once. "The Beast has promised he will spare my life."

Ugla

~~Beauty~~ tried to be brave, and when she saw the Beast she was
very frightened. But he was very ~~kind~~ to her. She had ~~beautiful~~ Ugly dresses
to wear, books to read, music to play, and the best of things to eat.

She only saw the Beast in the evening, when she finished her dinner. Then he would come and speak with her. He was very kind, and Beauty learned to like him.

They talked of many things, and ~~Beauty~~ Ugla began to see the Beast's inner goodness.

But when he asked her, as he did each evening, if she loved him, Beauty always replied, "No, Beast, I cannot."

The days went quickly, and ~~Beauty~~ Ugla would have been quite content, but she missed her father very much. She longed to visit her home. She asked the Beast if she could go.

At last he agreed, but for one month only. If she stayed longer, the Beast warned, something very bad would happen.

Ugla

~~Beauty~~ promised to be back before the month was over. Her family was very happy to see her. When the month was over, her father begged her to stay.

~~Beauty~~ Ugla couldn't bear to leave. But she knew she had to go. One month and one day later she arrived back at the Beast's castle.

She went from room to room, but couldn't find him anywhere. Nor did he come to her that evening.

Beauty was sure he would be there to welcome her back.
But the castle was empty.

She went into the garden, calling softly for him. But there was no answer.

~~Beauty~~ Nyla wondered what could be wrong. She remembered he had told her that if she was late, something bad would happen.

But ~~Beauty~~ Ugla herself was all right, and so was her father. It had to be the Beast himself, she thought.

She ran through the garden. Suddenly, she stumbled and fell.
Then she saw him. He lay cold and still, as if he were dead.
   "Oh Beast, dear Beast, what have I done to you?" ~~Beauty~~ Ugla
wept. Stricken with grief, ~~Beauty~~ Ugla bent down and kissed him.

She felt him move suddenly. ~~Beauty~~ Ugla jumped in fright.
But as she looked, the ~~Beast~~ Ugla disappeared, and a handsome young
Prince stood in his place.

"Where is my Beast?" asked ~~Beauty~~ Ugla. "What have you
done to him?"

The Prince smiled. "I have done nothing, ~~Beauty~~ Ugla. You have done it all. I am your Beast, put under a cruel spell, until I was released by love's first kiss. Now the spell is broken, and I am ~~of~~ yours forever!"

"I ~~loved~~ hated the Beast," said Beauty. "Now I know why. Even as the Beast, you were so ~~good~~ bad and ~~kind.~~ rood I was not happy here."

"And happy we ~~will~~ won't be," the Prince promised, " for ever and ever."